Mother Nature's Gifts

by Sara Levinson

Written by Sara Levinson

Illustrated by Charles Berton

Published by Butterfly Books

Visit Sara Levinson at: saralevinsonbooks.com

Visit Charles Berton at CharlesBerton.com

For Jason, Tabitha, Amory, and Kalista
for always playing outside with me.

Special thanks to:
My Mother and Aunt Sand
for making the many drives for us cousins to get
to play together and for teaching us the art of
being thankful for the simple pleasures in life;
and to Jeanne Quinn
for her constant belief in me and my work.
Alleluia!

This wonderful day at play has come to an end, so we tuck you in tight and say goodnight.

Off to dreamland you go, but just before you drift, thank Mother Nature for all her wonderful gifts.

I'll name just a few; it will take a moment or two, and it will remind you of your day and your fun time at play.

This day filled with friends, smiles, and fun, was brightened by Earth's beautiful sun.

Running barefoot through the grass and finding rocks that look like treasures,

are just a couple of nature's valuable pleasures.

Hearing the sounds of the animals and other children at play,

are more reminders of
this wonderful day.

A cool gust of wind helps your kite fly high in the air;

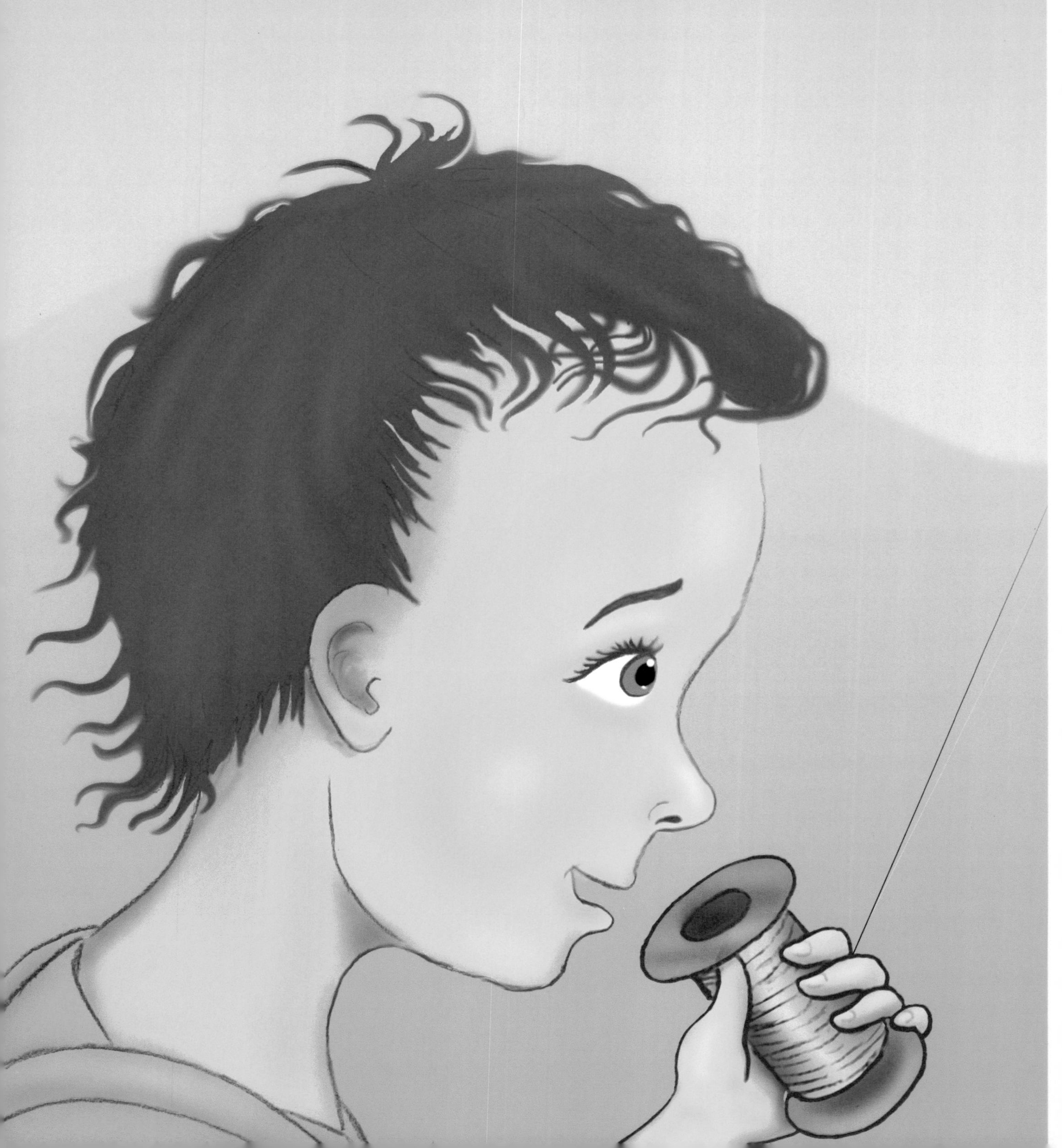

it cools your rosy cheeks
and plays with your hair.

At all of nature's many beauties
you must take a quick glance,

for the raindrops alone
have taught you to dance.

Every pile of leaves you dive into, every flower you pick, every puddle you splash and every snowball and stick,

are all part of Mother Earth we see each day, whose nature is here to help children play.

Now the moonlight shines and the stars sparkle above, tomorrow brings another magical day filled with laughter and love.

So it's off to dreamland you go, but just before you drift, thank Mother Nature for all her wonderful gifts.

About the Author

Sara Levinson is the proud author of Mother Nature's Gifts and three other children's books including Itty Bitty Bugs, When I Grow Up What Will I Be, and My Friend.

Sara is originally from Saint Louis, Missouri and graduated from the University of Missouri, Columbia with a degree in Psychology with an emphasis on Human Development and Family Study. As an avid lover of outdoor adventure and nature, she lived in Yosemite National Park for years enjoying rock climbing, hiking, and writing her children's books and poetry.

She currently works as a registered nurse and resides in California. You can find Sara's work at saralevinsonbooks.com and follow her on Twitter at @slevinsonbooks.

Made in the USA
Columbia, SC
03 June 2024